Little
Robin
Red Vest

For Birdie Black.
This one is for you x

First published 2018 by Nosy Crow Ltd
The Crow's Nest, 14 Baden Place, Crosby Row, London SE1 1YW
www.nosycrow.com

This edition published 2019

ISBN 978 1 78800 270 7

Nosy Crow and associated logos are trademarks
and/or registered trademarks of Nosy Crow Ltd.

Text and illustrations © Jan Fearnley 2018

A CIP catalogue record for this book is available from the British Library.

Printed in China
Papers used by Nosy Crow are made from wood grown in sustainable forests.

5 7 9 8 6 4

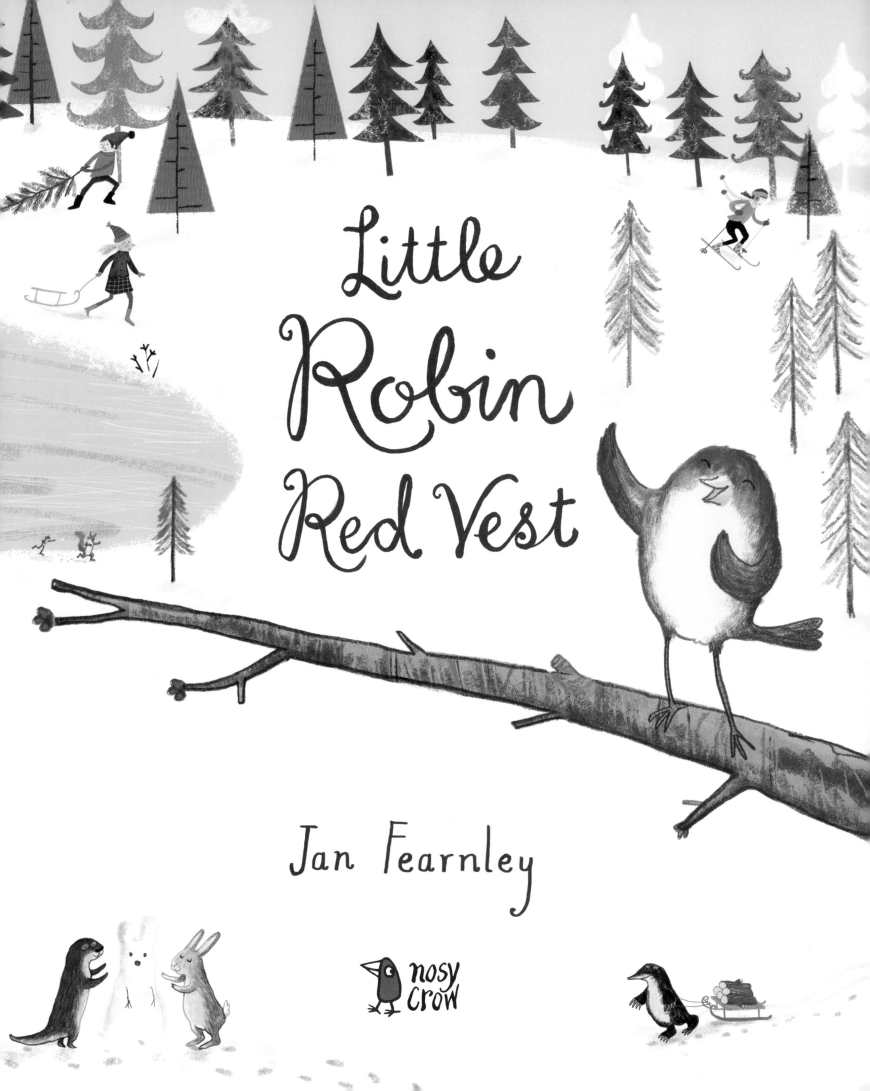

Little Robin Red Vest

Jan Fearnley

nosy crow

Once upon a time, there was a little brown bird.
His name was Robin, and this is his story.

It was the week before Christmas and Little Robin
was getting very excited. He washed and ironed
seven warm vests for the frosty days ahead.

He put on his white vest and
set out to skate on the pond.

On the way, he met Frog.

"I'm so cold!" said Frog.
"Can you help?"

Little Robin gave Frog his white vest.

"I've still got six vests left,"
he thought, as Frog hopped off happily.

Six days before Christmas, Little Robin put on his green vest and dashed out to play in the snow.

Down the path came Hedgehog. "I'm freezing!" she said.

Little Robin gave Hedgehog his green vest.

"I've still got **five** vests left," he thought,
waving goodbye to his prickly friend.

Five days before Christmas, Little Robin put on his pink vest and went to look for worms.

He hadn't gone far when Mole appeared.

"Brrrrrrr! The ground's too hard to dig, and I'm chilly!" he complained.

So Little Robin gave his pink vest to Mole.

It was a bit tight, but Mole didn't mind.
He was nice and warm.

"Four vests left," thought Little Robin.

Four days before Christmas, Little Robin
put on his yellow vest and flew up to sit
in the tall oak tree . . .

. . . where he met Squirrel.

"I'm so cold I can't sleep!"
Squirrel grumbled.

Little Robin handed over his yellow vest.

"Only **three** vests left now," he thought,
as Squirrel dozed off.

Three days before Christmas,
Little Robin put on his blue vest.

He was swooping down through the clouds
when he saw Rabbit on the hill.

"I'm so cold my teeth are chattering!"
shivered Rabbit.

Little Robin gave Rabbit his blue vest.

"Well, I've still got two vests left," he said to himself,
as Rabbit went cheerfully on his way.

Two days before Christmas, Little Robin put on his purple vest and skipped along the riverbank.

Next to the river stood Otter with her baby. She was very unhappy. "My baby is poorly!" she said.

Little Robin's purple vest was just right
for Baby Otter, and made him feel much better.

"Oh dear, I've only ONE vest left,"
thought Little Robin.

On the day before Christmas,
Little Robin put on his very
last vest, a warm, orange one.

He'd been walking and whistling to himself
for some time when he met a little mouse,
shivering in the garden.

Little Robin felt so sorry for her that he took off
his last woolly vest and pulled it over her chilly ears.

Now it was late on Christmas Eve, the snow
was falling and poor Little Robin had nothing
warm to wear.

There was nobody around to help him, and it was
a long way home. He fluffed up his feathers as best
he could and huddled miserably on a snowy roof.

Soon he fell fast asleep.
Not even the sleigh bells woke him . . .

. . . or the crunch of snow under two heavy black boots.

Large hands scooped Little Robin up and tucked him into a soft, white beard. "You had better come with me, my lad!" chuckled a gruff, jolly voice.

"This is the generous little fellow I told you
about," the man said to his wife.
"He must have a very special present then," she replied.

And, with Little Robin snug and cosy in her lap,
the lady set to work. She pulled a thread from a big,
bright red coat . . .

and with it she knitted a tiny vest.
It was a perfect fit for a little bird.

"I'm very proud of you," said the man with a smile.
"You gave away all your warm clothes to help
other people. You are full of the spirit of Christmas.
Now it's time for your present. This vest is very, very special.
It will keep you warm forever and when other people see you,
it will make them feel warm too."

It was time to go, back across the skies as the sun rose to kiss the land. Little Robin was very happy. His chest glowed as red as a reindeer's nose.

Soon Little Robin was home.

"Merry Christmas!" cried the man as he flew off.

"Goodbye, and thank you!" Little Robin shouted back.

It was Christmas morning. Boys and girls
everywhere were opening their presents.
Little Robin flew to the very highest branch,
proudly wearing his new red vest, and
sang out sweetly to wish everyone a

"Merry Christmas!"